The Kingfisher Jump

Beryl Reid

Illustrated by John Bendall-Brunello

BBC BOOKS

Andy the kitten was born on a fish farm in the village. He couldn't see much at first because his eyes were hardly open. He was very small and round and black.

When he got a bit bigger he used to sit and watch the fish. They were of beautiful colours and very elegant.

One day, when Andy was about ten weeks old, a
lovely lady called Carol drove up to the fish farm. She
talked to the man in charge, who smiled and nodded
his head.

Carol picked up the small, round bundle of fur. "Hello Andy," she whispered. "I'm going to take you to see Beryl," she said, "You'll like her. She lives at Honeypot Cottage, and that's to be your new home."

She put Andy into a basket, and on to the back seat of the car. They drove off.

Soon they arrived at Honeypot Cottage. Andy didn't even have time to cry a lot or feel sick.

Everyone made a great fuss of Andy, and rubbed his head a lot.

He played in the garden, but he could see the danger! He was told not to play by the stream at the bottom of the garden. But Andy was still fascinated by the fish.

Andy looked up at the butterflies that flitted about
in the garden, but they were too quick for him
to play with.

When he was tired of playing and having his head rubbed, Andy found a hole in the wall, where the coal was kept, and had a good sleep.

Andy was invisible there, because he was the same colour as the coal. Everyone said he was "Lost". After a good sleep he got up and stretched. He came out of the coal hole, and was what was called "Found".

Andy was very fond of jumping, but not very good at it . . . He practised everywhere. Indoors . . .

. . . and out.

In the kitchen one day, Andy tried to jump from the worktop to the fridge, which was very tall. But he missed the fridge, and landed among a lot of boxes. They fell everywhere. Andy was in disgrace.

He carried on jumping though. Small jumps at first,

then long jumps,

then high jumps.

Then very long jumps, and very high jumps.

Then sideways jumps and . . .

. . . one day, Andy did a very special jump.

And he caught a tiny bird, very carefully, in his mouth.
He carried it gently into the kitchen.

"Oh Andy, how clever you are," said Beryl, but she looked quite upset. She took the beautiful little bird out of his mouth and wrapped it in a pair of knickers from the linen basket.

She laid the parcel in a little box on the worktop. "You must have jumped very high to catch a bird like that," said Beryl to Andy.

Andy didn't know what to think about this. How could he be such a clever cat if Beryl looked so upset?

He went out into the garden again, to think about this.

A little while later, Beryl came out into the garden too. She was carrying something carefully in her hands.

"Andy!" she called, "Andy!"

Andy came rushing across the grass to see what she was holding.

Beryl undid the knicker-parcel, and the beautiful little bird flew away, as quick as light.

Everyone made a great fuss of Andy. "Oh Andy," they said, "You are clever . . .

. . . but naughty too! You mustn't do it again, because that lovely little bird was a kingfisher. You must have done the biggest and best jump you have ever done as the kingfisher is one of the fastest birds in the world!"

Andy ran off across the garden. He still didn't understand why he had been naughty and clever at the same time.

So he went off to sit on the coal and think. He wanted to be invisible again. "It's a good idea to be invisible," thought Andy, "When you want to have a good think!"

Published by BBC Books,
a division of BBC Enterprises Limited,
Woodlands, 80 Wood Lane, London W12 0TT
First published 1991
Text © Beryl Reid 1991
Illustrations © John Bendall-Brunello
ISBN 0 563 36181 6
Set in Baskerville Roman by Goodfellow & Egan, Cambridge
Printed and bound in Belgium by Proost N.V.
Colour separations by Dot Gradations Ltd., Chelmsford
Paper Case printed by Proost N.V.